Hoods

Hoods

Angela Betzien

Currency Press, Sydney

CURRENCY TEENAGE SERIES

First published in 2007
by Currency Press Pty Ltd,
PO Box 2287, Strawberry Hills, NSW, 2012, Australia.
enquiries@currency.com.au; www.currency.com.au

Reprinted 2009, 2010

NATIONAL LIBRARY OF AUSTRALIA CIP DATA
    Betzien, Angela, 1978–.
    Hoods.
    For secondary school students.
    ISBN 978 0 86819 800 2.
    1. Poverty–Drama. 2. Family violence–Drama. I. Title.
    A822.4

Publication of this title was assisted by the Commonwealth Government through the Australia Council, its arts funding and advisory body.

Contents

Introduction
    Noel Jordan and Robin Penty   vii

Author's Note   viii

Production Notes   xiii

HOODS   1

Biographies   41

Set for Currency Press by Dean Nottle.
Cover design by Kate Florance.
Cover shows Jodie Le Visconte and Christopher Sommers. Photograph by Daryl
Charles; copyright © Real TV, 2006.

Currency Press acknowledges the Traditional Owners of the Country on which
we live and work. We pay our respects to all Aboriginal and Torres Strait
Islander Elders, past and present.

Introduction

Angela Betzien is an exciting new voice creating compelling works for young audiences. Her work first came to our attention via her engrossing script, *Children of the Black Skirt* (2005). Angela's ability to capture the harrowing plight of children placed into institutional care throughout Australia's history powerfully affected the many young people who saw and read this work.

Sydney Opera House and Regional Arts Victoria are proud to be associated with the commissioning and development of *Hoods*. *Hoods* is a story of poverty, domestic violence and isolation set against the backdrop of a suburban landscape. The premise is simple and immediate. As night falls, Kyle and Jessie wait in a car for their mother while nursing their crying baby brother. As glimpsed fleetingly through the car window, the action masterfully switches perspective from the two children to a multitude of characters from their lives, often at breakneck speed. Time and space are manipulated and unravelled to reveal potential sources of hope: the children's grandmother or Jessie's favourite teacher are juxtaposed dramatically with real threats of danger, including the advances of a predatory stranger in a twenty-four-hour convenience store.

This is perhaps the greatest strength of Angela's writing—the ability to vividly create a variety of believable characters and situations that inhabit the periphery of the central characters' lives. Betzien embraces non-naturalism and in the process, rather than alienating her audience, captivates us and draws us in. The result is a confronting and poignant contemporary tale of 'lost children' in a fight for survival and solidarity against the odds.

Noel Jordan
Producer, Young Audiences
Sydney Opera House

Robin Penty
Producer and Education Program Manager
Regional Arts Victoria

Author's Note

I started to write this play several years ago. The initial idea: three kids in a dirty white Kingswood abandoned in a carpark. I had in my head an image of a baby wrapped in a wet newspaper nappy. At some point in the writing I looked over and saw a man with a lighter in his hand sitting in an orange Datsun in the distant carpark. I became distracted and ended up telling that character's story in another play called *Playboy of the Working Class*. I returned to the story of these kids when I began work on a collection of short plays inspired by the political theatre tradition of Living Newspaper. Living Newspaper was first used in Russia, primarily as a means of communicating the news to a population that was largely illiterate. In the 1930s during the Depression in the United States, Living Newspaper was again utilised by companies formed under the Federal Theatre Project, a massive visionary government effort to support thousands of unemployed theatre artists. I'm interested in exploring a contemporary approach to Living Newspaper, creating theatre which deals with the Australian experience, particularly with the stories of those from our underclass, the alienated and the oppressed. This play is inspired by many actual, though non-specific incidents of children who have been left in cars, abandoned by their parents for hours at a time. Often this parental neglect is the result of drug, alcohol or gambling addictions, which are side effects of social and economic disadvantage.

Hoods is a reworking of *Kingswood Kids*, an earlier play of mine. *Kingswood Kids* was first presented by Real TV as part of De Base Productions' Sheilas' Shorts Festival at Metro Arts in 2001. Based on the huge success of this production it was subsequently programmed as part of La Boite Theatre's 2002 season.

During the season at La Boite Theatre several members of the audience walked out, crossing the stage area to do so. Questioned by the front of house staff outside, these people said the play was too dark, too emotionally draining. Several groups of high school students who attended a performance of the play were similarly affected, however they were thrilled by it as well. They loved the theatricality, intensity and familiarity of the play's form and content. The responses from these young people awoke the possibility that the play could be adapted for touring to high schools. Real TV felt very strongly that issues of poverty, consumerism and violence were particularly relevant to young people. The challenge would be to communicate these issues in a way that distanced both the actor and audience from the emotionally dark and intense aspects of the story and to incorporate the element of hope and possibility.

In 2004, Real TV initiated the process of adapting *Kingswood Kids* for high school audiences. The text underwent three creative development phases throughout 2005, two of which took place in Rockhampton at Central Queensland University, as part of the Drama Department's Artists' Residency program. In the first phase, the writer and the director workshopped the original text with second-year Drama students and their lecturer Howard Cassidy. The second creative development also took place in Rockhampton, culminating in a 'work in progress' performance by the same CQU second-year Drama students for an audience of middle and high school students from Rockhampton. This process, which included gathering feedback from the audience, informed a radically new version of the text. *Hoods* was written to be performed by two actors and toured to high schools. In May 2005, Real TV presented a rehearsed reading of *Hoods* to domestic violence workers, police, high school students and members of the community as part of Domestic Violence Awareness Month. This creative development was supported by North Side Alliance Against Domestic Violence.

The production of *Hoods* was subsequently commissioned by Regional Arts Victoria Arts2GO and Sydney Opera House:Ed.

The work was also supported by the Queensland Department of Communities and Families. Jess Wilson, Principal Program Officer in the Department of Communities, Violence Prevention Team, was on board to ensure that the issues raised in the script were addressed sensitively. During the Queensland metropolitan tour of the play the Department of Communities provided a Child Witness Counsellor who was on hand after each performance to debrief the young audience and offer support and advice to students who may be at risk.

Hoods has been seen by over ten thousand young people across Australia and will continue to tour schools in the years to come.

Violence and addiction have a devastating and often invisible impact on our society, particularly on children. These are deep social and political issues that I believe can only really be addressed through radical change. Silence and suppression will never be the solution, solidarity is.

Angela Betzien
Melbourne, January 2007

First Production

Hoods was commissioned by Sydney Opera House:Ed and Regional Arts Victoria Arts2GO. It premiered at the Sydney Opera House Studio on 8 May 2006 with the following cast:

Jodie Le Vesconte	Jessie
Christopher Sommers	Kyle

Director, Leticia Cáceres
Composer, Pete Goodwin
Designer, Jonathon Oxlade
Lighting Designer, Glenn Hughes
Stage Manager, Kylie Mitchell

Acknowledgements

Howard Cassidy, University of Central Queensland 2005 second-year Drama students, Joan Cassidy, Yepoon State High School, Paul Betzien, Jodie Le Vesconte, Christopher Sommers, Samantha Betzien, Sebastian Bourges, Jody Betzien, Helen Weder, Gail Hargraves, Lisa Berlin, North Side Alliance Against Domestic Violence, Erin Milne, Louise Brehmer, Scott Witt, Queensland Theatre Company, Visible Ink, Adrianne Jones, Corin Edwards, Janette Bruvel, Helen Strube, Rebecca Shearman, Jess Wilson, the Department of Communities and Families, Noel Jordan, Mia Bucholtz, Nan Weder, Kylie Mitchell, Leticia Cáceres, Jonathon Oxlade, Glenn Hughes, Pete Goodwin, Robin Penty, Hellene Workman, Jim Lawson, Drama Victoria, Arena Theatre, Michael Wheelan, Queensland Arts Council, Amy Trotman, 2005 QUT Masters Cohort, Laurel Collins, Marcel Dorney, Marc Richards, Judy Couttie, Sean Mee.

Photographs by Daryl Charles; copyright © Real TV 2006.

For further information about Angela Betzien or Real TV contact:
www.realtv.net.au
or email Angela Betzien: angelabetzien@realtv.net.au

Production Notes

Hoods has been written to be performed by two actors—one male and one female. Throughout the play, the actors 'morph' into multiple characters. The word morph is used throughout the text to describe the actors' rapid vocal and physical transformation from one character to the next. The Hoods characters are manifested when the actors pull their hooded jumpers over their heads.

In Real TV's touring production the set is a simple, versatile design intended to conjure the landscape of a wrecking yard on the outskirts of a city. Through the poetic narration of the Hoods the set is transformed into a variety of other locations including a shopping centre carpark, Kmart, a classroom, a flat and a twenty-four-hour convenience store. Props are kept to a minimum. Baby Troy is represented by a doll.

The play employs a video game structure. The story of Kyle, Jessie and Troy is a game the Hoods play. The Hoods pause, replay and fast forward the action as they tell the tale of a particular car.

The rhymed narration is shared by the Hoods characters. This heightened language has been influenced by the tradition of spoken word. When performing these characters I would encourage experimentation with the language. The performer may like to consider the use of onomatopoeia, staccato, elongated consonants and rhythm. The layout of the language is designed to assist the performer with this experimentation.

It is possible to produce the play using an ensemble of actors. It would also be possible to improvise and/or write other characters who may meet and interact with the kids in the carpark.

Our world is changing at a rapid rate so feel free to update the popular culture references in the text such as Xbox 360 and Warcraft when they become outdated.

Characters

Hoods, two hooded homeless kids
Joyriders
Old Couple
Jessie, a girl aged nine
Kyle, a boy aged eleven
Troy, an eleven-month-old baby represented by a doll found in the wrecked car
Mum, Jessie's and Kyle's mum
Mother
Child
Homeless Man
Older Woman
Skateboarder
Security Guard 1
Man in Thongs
Cashier at Kmart
Young Woman
Security Guard 2
Mr Matheson, Jessie's teacher
Mrs Muir, Kyle's teacher
Kid, a student in Kyle's class
Dealer
Social Worker
Nightowl Man

Two hooded figures wait on a suburban train platform.

Hoods   Two Hoods.
    A suburban train station.
    Above us the constellations
    spin and burn.
    No tickets for we are ghosts of past present and future.
    We sew the sutures
    of time.
    We are the game players
    controllers
    of fast forward pause and rewind.

    Express train Eagle Junction to Beenleigh.
    Keenly
    we board the loneliest carriage.
    An old man mutters madness into his multiple chins
    raving repent repent or burn for your sins.

    Train shunts through the dark
    slows to a
    snail's
    pace
    past pylons thick with tagging
    then speeds up screaming along its sharp silver splints.
    The tags become a silent motion picture
    like the handprints on ancient cave walls
    trying to teach the illiterate
    who obliterate
    their language.
    Lights flicker on and off
    breath stops.
    For a second
    time
    is
    suspended.

Beenleigh station
trains termination.
Midnight.
Hands in pockets
heads down
us two Hoods alight
and
take
flight.

The HOODS run through the suburban streets.

We catch our breath
let the lungs in our chests
rest.
Then
he burrows under the steely defence of the fence.
She springs over
narrowly escaping the hungry teeth of barbed wire
keeping junk from wandering
Hoods like us from trespassing
this wrecking yard.
This cemetery of stories
this mortuary of memory
where the rusted carcasses of cars
all commemorate a story.
Where each object abandoned
in the glovebox
or the boot
smothered in the ashtray
or loot
wedged behind the passenger seat
coughs up a recollection
of an interaction
a happening.

Such as
this hooned-up Gemini.

The HOODS discover two beer cans on the floor of the wrecked Gemini.

They morph into JOYRIDERS speeding in a stolen car.

The sound of a police siren.

Joyriders Cops cops cops!

The Gemini veers off the road.

Tree tree tree!

The JOYRIDERS morph back into the HOODS.

Hoods Exit game.

The HOODS find another car in the yard.

Such as
this gutted green Austin.

The HOODS find an old lady's straw hat wedged in the seat of the green Austin.

Load game.
Play game.

'... this hooned-up Gemini'

The HOODS morph into an ELDERLY COUPLE singing along as they drive at a snail's pace.

Old Man Look out for the pedestrian!

The OLD LADY beeps the horn.

Old Lady They can bloody look out for me!

The OLD COUPLE morph back into the HOODS.

Hoods Exit game.

One of the HOODS yawns.

The sound of a dog's ferocious bark.

Hark.
A dog barks in the dark.
The pitbull has registered our presence
and through this minefield of machinery
pursues us with all of its senses
until it gets a whiff
sniffs cat's piss
and tears off in another direction.

The HOODS are chased by the pitbull through the wrecking yard. They find themselves inside a car.

What mechanical corpse
have we crawled in?
We check it out.
It's a rusty four-door
Commodore.

The HOODS explore the car. They find a large bag, in it a cap, an empty packet of chips, assorted clothing, a plastic bag.

They find a doll.

Now
it's time.
Let this Commodore speak more.
Load game.

They sit in the car, ready to play.

Play game.

Set 5.05 a.m.

The HOODS morph into KYLE and JESSIE asleep in the car.

A sound like a gunshot wakes JESSIE. Clutching a baby, she creeps out of the car and wanders toward the darkness.

KYLE wakes, notices JESSIE leaving and struggles out of the car.

Jessie We gotta go.
Kyle Where's Mum?
Jessie We gotta go.
Kyle Where's Mum?
Jessie Mum's gone.

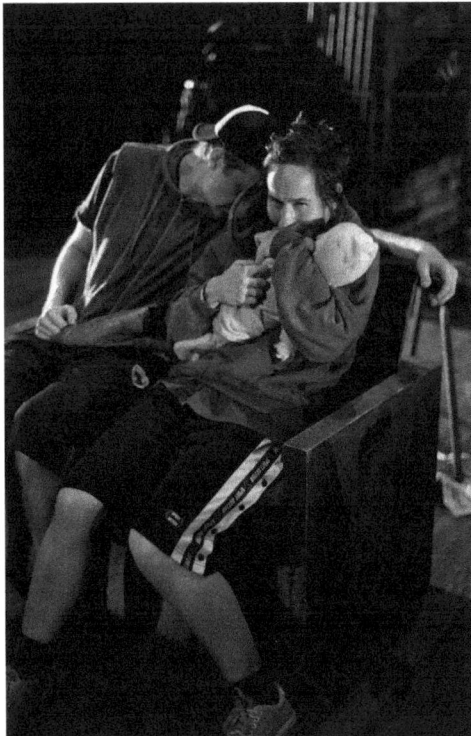

Kyle wakes.

Kyle Where's she gone?

Jessie The baby's cold.

Kyle Where's she gone? Where's she gone?

Jessie We gotta go.

Kyle We gotta wait for Mum.

Jessie Kyle, come on, we gotta go. The baby's cold.

Kyle Can't leave Mum. What if she comes back?

Jessie We'll leave a trail. She'll follow us to Nan's.

> *JESSIE takes a chip packet from her pocket and makes a trail of chips leading into the dark.*

Come on, Kyle. Come on.

Kyle Jessie, you get back in the car.

Jessie I'm goin', Kyle. Come on.

> *KYLE takes a plastic bag out of his shorts pocket.*

Kyle Jessie, you leave. Jessie, you leave…

> *He pulls the plastic bag over his head.*

Jessie What's that? That's not funny Kyle. Kyle, take it off. That's not funny Kyle. Take it off. Take it off.

> *JESSIE returns to the car. She places the baby back in his car seat.*

I'll stay in the car, Kyle. I'll stay in the car. Take it off.

> *They sit in the darkness of the car, silent and waiting.*

> *JESSIE and KYLE morph into the HOODS.*

Hoods Pause.

This is what happened.

The constellations disappear.

It is the sun's turn to rise and burn the skies.

The windscreen morphs into a magnifying glass fast
raising the temperature inside the car.

A cleaner on her way to work walks past
finds three bodies entwined
camped out in a Commodore.

Sirens sing their emergency hymn
warning the early morning.

The ambulance arrives
prises open the door.
The baby has died.

Exit game.
Save game.
Replay.
Three-forty p.m. yesterday.

> *One of the HOODS morphs into MUM, the other KYLE. The KIDS are mucking up in the back seat.*

Mum Kids!

> *Silence.*

I'm just going to get a few things. Look after the baby. Stay in the car.

> *MUM morphs into JESSIE sitting in the back seat. KYLE and JESSIE watch MUM as she heads into the shopping centre.*

> *JESSIE nurses baby Troy.*

Jessie I spy with my little eye somethin' beginnin' with… S. Kyle?

> *JESSIE waits for an answer but KYLE is preoccupied playing imaginary computer games.*

Didn't ya hear me? I spy with my little eye somethin' beginnin' with S. Kyle? Somethin' beginnin' with S.

> *She waits for a response.*

No, not supermarket.

> *She waits for a response.*

Not Sizzla. Wish we was goin' to Sizzla. Don't you Kyle?

Kyle We're havin' KFC.

Jessie Yeah, but don't you wish we was goin' to Sizzla tonight?

> *She waits.*

Wanna hint?

> *She mimes playing Playstation.*

Ya give up? Kyle? Ya give up? Sony Playstation.

KYLE presses his face against the window of the car.

Kyle Where?

Jessie In that trolley there.

KYLE and JESSIE morph into MOTHER with CHILD.

Mother Where were you?

Child Looking at toys.

The CHILD sulks.

Mother Get in the car. I said get in the car. Do you want a slap? Do you? You keep this up, Brittany, you won't get a bloody thing from Santa this year.

'I spy...'

MOTHER and CHILD morph back into KYLE and JESSIE.

Kyle That's an Xbox 360.

Jessie Hoh.

Kyle That Xbox'd be for Christmas.

Jessie Yeah.

Kyle Wish I was an Xbox wish I was.

Jessie Wish I was a Barbie Princess wish I was.

Pause.

Who's that, Kyle? That Santa?

Kyle Where?

Jessie Over there.

JESSIE morphs into a HOMELESS MAN.

Homeless Man Two bucks? Please, two bucks, for a meal, for a bus?

The HOMELESS MAN approaches the KIDS in the car.

You kids got two bucks, for a meal, for a bus?

KYLE loads an imaginary bazooka and launches a missile at the HOMELESS MAN.

The HOMELESS MAN is blasted away.

The HOMELESS MAN rises up and returns to the car.

Jus' two bucks. Please, for a meal, for a bus?

KYLE reloads the bazooka and fires.

The HOMELESS MAN is destroyed.

The HOMELESS MAN rises up and shuffles away.

Kyle Kyle wins three hundred points. Replay.

The HOMELESS MAN morphs back into JESSIE in the car.

Replay.

Jessie Kyle, I need a pee.

KYLE ignores JESSIE.

The KIDS see an OLDER WOMAN loading shopping into her car.

There's Nan.

Kyle   Where?

Jessie   Over there.

> *JESSIE morphs into the OLDER WOMAN.*
>
> *She lights a cigarette and smokes it. She has a coughing attack.*
>
> *The OLDER WOMAN notices the KIDS.*

Older Woman   Hello.

> *The KIDS don't respond.*

Kyle   It's not Nan.

Older Woman   You kids all right?

Kyle   Don't talk to her, Jessie.

> *The OLDER WOMAN rummages through her shopping bags and finds a chocolate bar. She offers it to the KIDS.*

Older Woman   You want this? I shouldn't have it, goes straight to me hips.

Kyle   Mum said, Jessie.

Older Woman   All right, suit yourselves. See ya then.

> *The OLDER WOMAN morphs back into JESSIE.*

Jessie   Looked like Nan.

Kyle   She's miles away.

Jessie   Look, Kyle, there's Dad. Kyle? There's Dad.

> *KYLE looks, then morphs into a SKATERBOARDER doing ollies in the carpark.*
>
> *JESSIE morphs into the shopping centre SECURITY GUARD.*

Security Guard 1   Hey.

> *The SKATERBOARDER ignores him.*

Hey, can you read?

Skateboarder   What do you reckon?

Security Guard 1   I reckon you're too thick, otherwise you'd have read that sign over there that says skateboarding is prohibited in this carpark. If I see you here again I'll call the police.

Skateboarder   Yeah? Well, I'll kick your head in.

Security Guard 1 Aren't you a bit old for kids' games?
Skateboarder Get—

> *The SECURITY GUARD and SKATEBOARDER morph back into KYLE and JESSIE in the car.*

Jessie That's not Dad.
Kyle Dad's got a better board than that.

> *Pause.*

Jessie Kyle, I need a pee.
Kyle Bet I'm missin' 'Neighbours'. Bet I am.
Jessie I got an idea. Kyle, I got an idea.

> *She mimes switching the television on, the screen is the window of the car.*

It's nearly on. Kyle, 'Neighbours' is nearly on. Kyle, I'm watchin' the tele. It's just the weather now. It's gunna snow tomorrow. Kyle, they says it's gunna snow tomorrow. Kyle, 'Neighbours' is on now.

> *She hums along with the theme tune.*

Kyle? Ya missin' it.

> *KYLE stares out the window aiming and shooting his weapons at passersby.*

Kyle, ya missin' it.

> *KYLE blows apart JESSIE's pretend TV with his pretend weapon.*

Ya missed it.

> *JESSIE notices a MAN on a mobile phone.*

Hey Kyle, isn't that Dad's friend?
Kyle Who?
Jessie Yer know, Dad's best friend with the thongs who always comes over?
Kyle Mick? Where?

> *KYLE morphs into a MAN wearing thongs, who is talking on a mobile phone.*

Man In Thongs I dunno I dunno where he is he said seven he said seven he's not here he said seven I dunno I dunno I said I dunno in the carpark in the carpark he said in the carpark outside Kmart at seven he said seven what do I do what do I do?

JESSIE waves at the MAN.

Jessie Mick?

The MAN morphs back into KYLE.

Kyle It's not Mick.
Jessie He talks like Mick.
Kyle Shut ya mouth.

In the carpark.

Pause.

Jessie What'll Mum bring back ya think Kyle?
Kyle Nikes.
Jessie Will not.

KYLE and JESSIE morph into the HOODS.

Hoods Pause.
Rewind.
Late-night shopping
K-Mart.
The teenager with the moon-crater face
farts
croaks an order
over the loudspeaker
price check on weedkiller
wishing he was at home
on the computer
playing 'Warcraft'.
The manager
detecting his lack of enthusiasm
for late-night shifts
parts his lips
spits
threatens to cut his hours in half.
A child in the toy section
itching
needing a dose of Combantrim
chucks a tantrum
demands a remote-control car.
A crotchety lady in chiffon
standing in line
claims a refund
for a giant pack
of expired Snickers bars.

One of the HOODS morphs into MUM.

Throughout the scene, the HOOD playing MUM morphs back and forth into JESSIE.

Mum Here, Kyle, try 'em on.

MUM hands a pair of Dunlops to KYLE.

Kyle Wanna pair o' Nikes.

Mum No you don't.

Jessie Mum, can me 'n' Troy go look at the toys?

Mum We don't have time, Jess. Kyle, try 'em on quick.

Jessie Please, Mum?

Mum No, love.

Jessie Mum?

Mum I said no.

Jessie Please?

Mum Jessie, what did I say? Oh, Kyle, you look good in them.

Kyle Don't fit, none of 'em fit.

Mum You can grow into 'em.

Jessie Pleeeease can we go look at the toys?

Mum Jessie, I'm warning you.

Kyle Wanna pair o' Nikes.

Jessie Jus' wanna look.

Mum Come on you lot we're goin'.

KYLE morphs into a Kmart checkout CASHIER.

Cashier Declined.

Mum What?

Cashier Your card has been declined.

Jessie Mum, can we have a packet of Nerds?

Mum Try it again.

Cashier Declined.

Jessie Please, Mum?

Mum I got paid today.

Jessie Please, Mum, can we have a packet of Nerds?

Mum Hang on.

MUM empties her purse and counts out the coins.

Kyle Don't worry about it, Mum.

She continues counting.

Jessie Mum, pleeeeeeeeese.

Mum Shut up Jessie. Just shut up!

Silence.

MUM looks around. The other shoppers are staring.

What are youse lookin' at? Eh? Mind yer own business. We're all right. Come on kids let's go. Come on.

The characters morph back into KYLE and JESSIE in the car.

Silence.

Kyle Not wearin' any shoes 'til I get Nikes.

Jessie That's not fair. How come you get Nikes?

Kyle Fat girls can't wear Nikes. That's what Mum says. Mum says ya too fat for Nikes.

Pause.

Jessie There's Mum. Kyle, there's Mum.

Kyle Where?

Jessie Over there, with that security guard.

KYLE and JESSIE morph into a YOUNG WOMAN and a SECURITY GUARD.

The SECURITY GUARD is searching through the YOUNG WOMAN's handbag.

He pulls out a stolen item and shows it to her.

Young Woman Don't know what that's doing there.

Security Guard 2 What about the deodorant?

Young Woman Bought it at another shop.

Security Guard 2 And the lipstick?

Young Woman Got a job interview tomorrow.

Security Guard 2 Not anymore.

As the SECURITY GUARD leads the YOUNG WOMAN away, they morph back into KYLE and JESSIE in the car.

Kyle That's not Mum.

Jessie Yeah nuh.

Pause.

Kyle, I need a pee. Kyle, I need a go 'n' pee.

Pause.

There's me teacher. Mr Mafeson! Mr Mafeson! Mr Mafeson!

JESSIE and KYLE morph into the HOODS.

Hoods Pause.
High-speed diversion
Australia Zoo
school excursion
where cuteness is currency
and crocodiles keep curious crowds coming.
Tourists speaking alien tongues
flutter their digital shutters
stealing snapshots of
kiddy-cuddling
koalas.

The HOODS morph into JESSIE and MR MATHESON.

Jessie Mr Mafeson! Mr Mafeson, I wanna give you a hug.

Mr Matheson How about a handshake?

Jessie Nup, I wanna give you a hug.

Mr Matheson You can give me a cuddly handshake.

Jessie Okay.

They shake hands.

Mr Matheson It's boiling, Jessie. Don't you get hot wearing your jumper all day?

Jessie Nup. Koala bears wear their jumpers all day. They're not hot, they're cold. I'm cold most of the day. Me jumper's givin' me a hug.

Mr Matheson All right.

Jessie Feel sad if I got me jumper off.

MR MATHESON morphs back into KYLE in the car. JESSIE is calling after MR MATHESON in the carpark.

Mr Mafeson! Mr Mafeson!

> *Pause.*

He didn't see us. I love me teacher. Gunna miss Mr Mafeson on the holidays.

Kyle I hate me teacher. Hope Miss Muir dies on the holidays. One day I'm gunna chop her head off with some school scissors.

Jessie I need a pee. Kyle, I need to go 'n' pee. Kyle?

Kyle Shut up.

Jessie Kyle, I really really need a pee.

Kyle Go on then.

Jessie Wha'?

Kyle Go on.

Jessie By meself?

Kyle I'm not comin'.

Jessie Can you come with me, Kyle? We might see Mum.

> *Pause.*

Kyle Come on.

Jessie We can't leave Troy in the car, Kyle.

Kyle Yes we can.

Jessie No we can't, Kyle. We gotta bring him with us.

> *JESSIE collects Troy from the baby seat.*

Kyle Come on, it's closin'. Come on, Jessie.

> *The KIDS run to the supermarket but the automatic doors are locked. The shopping centre has closed.*

It's shut.

Jessie Kyle, I needa pee.

Kyle Shut ya mouth.

Jessie What'll Mum bring back ya think, Kyle?

Kyle Jessie, get back in the car.

> *They sit in silence, then fall asleep.*
>
> *A sound like a gunshot wakes them both suddenly.*

Jessie Where's Mum? Kyle, where's Mum? Think I peed me pants.

JESSIE morphs into a HOOD.

Hoods Pause.

Insert Special Feature.

Play.

Kyle Dear Journal, The title of me story is 'The Cat'. One day I was ridin' along the highway near me house. I saw a bag that was movin'. In it was a cat with hair all sticky and with one eye. I fed it KFC leftovers 'n' some milk from me Fruit Loops for breakfast. At night I kep' the cat in me bed with me. I liked the way me cat's body was warm 'n' movin'. One day me dad found me cat and took him outside. He smashed me cat with the shovel on the grass.

KYLE takes a plastic bag from his shorts pocket. He stares inside the bag.

Sometimes I wanna crawl inside me cat's bag 'n' go to sleep.

Troy is crying.

Paww! What stinks?

The shopping centre closes.

Jessie Troy's poo is all runny.

Kyle Chuck it out the window.

Jessie There's no more nappies left, Kyle.

Kyle Troy's got runny, smelly shit.

Jessie What'll I put him in?

Kyle Ya stink, Troy, do ya know that?

KYLE and JESSIE morph into the HOODS.

Hoods Pause.
Rewinding.
Tuesday morning.
Mrs Muir orders
silent group work in separate corners
while with hawk eye
she stalks the room.

One of the HOODS morphs into Kyle's teacher, MRS MUIR.

Mrs Muir What stinks in here? Smells like dead cat in this classroom. Kyle Johnson, have you had a bath this year? Look at you, you're filthy. Oh, go away, in the corner.

MRS MUIR morphs into a KID in Kyle's class.

Kid Ya stink povo, do ya know that?

KYLE goes to punch the KID.

Mrs Muir Kyle Johnson! I said silent group work.

KYLE takes the plastic cat's bag out of his pocket and pulls it over his head.

The KID morphs back into MRS MUIR.

Take that off. Kyle, I said take that off your head immediately. Do you want to see the principal? Kyle Johnson? Kyle!

MRS MUIR morphs back into JESSIE, in the car with KYLE.

Jessie Kyle? Can I wrap him in some newspaper? Jus' 'til Mum gets back?

JESSIE wraps Troy in a nappy of newspaper.

KYLE stares out the window.

There's a car over there. There's a man in it. We should ask him for help. I'm gonna ask him.

Kyle You move, Jessie... We gotta stay in the car like Mum said.

KYLE morphs into a DEALER who is on his mobile phone.

Dealer What's the point of havin' a dog if I gotta bark meself? Get the stuff here and get it here now.

The DEALER sees the KIDS in the car.

What are you lookin' at?

The DEALER morphs back into KYLE.

Kyle Prob'ly some killer. Prob'ly eats little kids. Prob'ly got some kid in his boot right now. Two maybe, if they're small enough. Three maybe, if they're preschoolers. Prob'ly feeds 'em up 'n' eats 'em. We listen, we'll hear 'em. Hear that, Jessie?

Jessie Nuh.

Kyle Hear that?

Jessie Nuh.

Kyle That's the preschooler's bony hands beatin' against the boot.

Jessie Don't scare us.

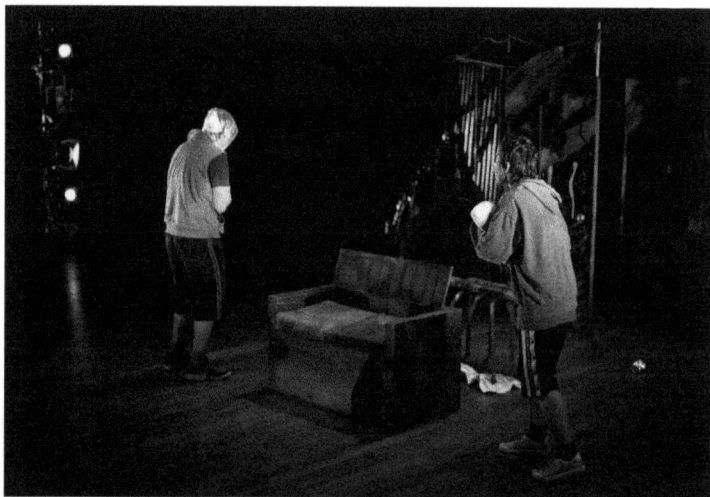

'Take that off...'

Kyle   Wish Troy'd shut up.

     KYLE yells in Troy's face.

  Shut up, Troy. Shut up. Shutuuuup!

Jessie   He's all right, Kyle. He's all right.

     The baby continues to cry.

Kyle   Let's put him in the boot.

Jessie   No, Kyle.

Kyle   Yeah, let's put him in the boot.

     Pause.

  Put him in the boot. Put him in the boot. Put him in the boot.

     KYLE snatches at Troy.

Jessie   No, Kyle.

     JESSIE throws a punch at KYLE.

     KYLE and JESSIE fight in video game style.

     JESSIE breaks free and runs into the darkness.

Kyle   Mum said to stay in the car, Jessie.

     He stares into the dark where JESSIE has gone.

  Jessie.

Jessie   Say ya sorry.

Kyle   Troy's cryin'.

Jessie   Say ya sorry.

Kyle   Troy's cryin'.

     Long pause.

     JESSIE suddenly runs back into the light. She is frightened by the dark.

     She quickly hops into the car and nurses Troy.

  We're all right, Jessie. We're just waitin' in the car for Mum.

     Long pause.

Jessie   'Member that time Dad left us in the car, Kyle? He went into that house 'n' didn't come back. 'Member that? He fell asleep 'n' forgot us. Mum hadda come get us. That was so funny. Wasn't it,

Kyle? Wasn't it funny? Dad bought us a Happy Meal. Didn't he, Kyle? Ya think Mum'll bring us a Happy Meal when she gets back? Or KFC? It's KFC night tonight. Isn't it, Kyle? Isn't it?

Kyle Shut ya mouth.

KYLE discovers a cigarette packet under the car seat. He finds a cigarette in it and lights it.

JESSIE looks at the packet.

Jessie This says these kill kids. Troy's got hot skin. He's hot all over. Maybe he's sick. Maybe he wants an iceblock. Yeah, he does. Let's go buy Troy an iceblock.

Kyle Take ya jumper off, then.

Jessie What?

Kyle Take ya jumper off, it's hot.

Jessie No, I'm not hot. Troy's hot. I'm cold. I'm freezin'. I been cold all day, that's why I got me jumper on. It might snow. Wouldn't it be nice if it snowed?

Kyle Stupid, it's summer.

Jessie Still, it might. It's Christmas time. That could happen.

Kyle Never snows.

Jessie Still, it could happen. It could.

Kyle Take ya jumper off.

Jessie It's snowing, Kyle. It's snowing.

JESSIE and KYLE morph into the HOODS.

Hoods Backtrack.
Wednesday afternoon
art and craft.
Making paddle pops wands
with glitter and Clag glue.
Plucked out of class
sitting in the counsellor's office
jumper soaked through
knees stained with grass.

Throughout this scene, one of the HOODS morphs back and forth from the SOCIAL WORKER to KYLE.

'It's snowing, Kyle.'

Kyle Don't talk to 'em, Jessie. Dad said.

Jessie You look like Ken.

Social Worker Thank you, I think.

Jessie Can you take us out of maths tomorrow?

Social Worker I can't do that.

Jessie Why not?

Social Worker I have to be somewhere else.

Jessie Where?

Social Worker I have to visit another family.

Jessie Why?

Social Worker That's my job. I visit families and make sure they're all right. Are you all right, Jessie?

> *JESSIE nods.*

Is Kyle all right?

> *JESSIE shrugs.*

How 'bout your mum? Is she all right?

Kyle Shut up, Jessie.

Jessie Do ya have kids?

Social Worker Yes.

Jessie Can I play with 'em? How old are they? Would they like me?

Kyle Jessie, don't talk to 'em.

Social Worker I'm sure they would.

Jessie Will you take me 'n' Kyle to Seaworld on the weekend?

Kyle Jessie, Dad said don't talk to 'em.

Social Worker I'm sorry, I can't.

Jessie Dreamworld?

Social Worker No.

Jessie Movieworld?

Social Worker No.

Jessie Wet 'n' Wild World?

Social Worker I'm sorry, Jessie, I can't.

Jessie Can I sleep over at your place on Friday night?

Social Worker Why don't you want to sleep at your house?

Kyle Shut ya mouth, Jessie.

Social Worker That's a pretty jumper you're wearing, Jessie.

    JESSIE is silent.

You wear it a lot. You must really love it.

    JESSIE is silent.

Tell me, do you ever take it off?

    JESSIE is silent.

Jessie?

    JESSIE shrinks away.

Jessie?

    JESSIE and the SOCIAL WORKER morph back into KYLE and JESSIE in the car.

Kyle Take ya jumper off!

    KYLE rips the jumper off JESSIE.

    JESSIE screams and cowers on the floor of the car.

Jessie I'm cold. It's been cold today. That's why I got me jumper on.

    Pause.

It's all right, Kyle. I know ya love me really.

Kyle Hate ya.

Jessie No ya don't.

Kyle Whinge.

Jessie Ya love me.

Kyle Never shut up.

Jessie You used to sing to me.

Kyle Don't know no songs.

Jessie 'Neighbours…'

    JESSIE sings the 'Neighbours' theme song.

    KYLE throws JESSIE's jumper into the back seat.

    JESSIE quickly puts it back on.

    JESSIE continues with the song.

    KYLE has fallen asleep.

It's all right, Kyle, I know you love me really.

> *The KIDS have both fallen asleep.*
>
> *The KIDS morph into the HOODS.*

Hoods Suburb's dark
street lights broken
safety forsaken
for some other council task.
One a.m.
kids in the car
they
sleep
masked
by night's thick blanket.

> *The HOODS morph back into JESSIE and KYLE asleep in the car.*
>
> *They wake to the sound of a loud noise like a gunshot.*
>
> *They sit silently in the car.*

Jessie It's the first day of the holidays, Kyle.

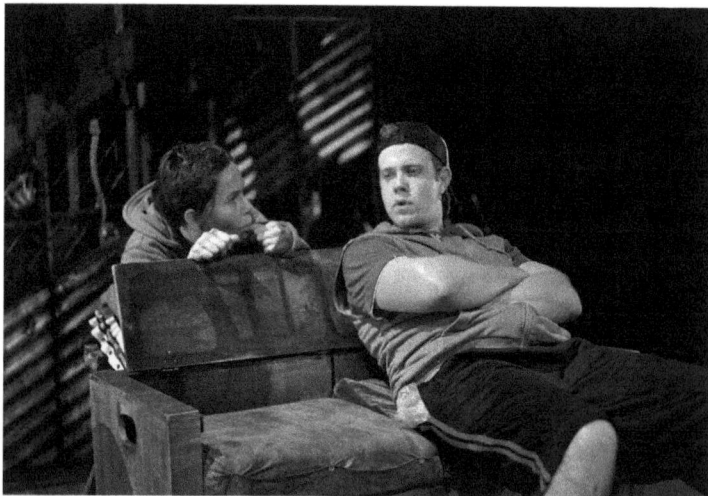

'It's the first day of the holidays, Kyle.'

Kyle So what? Not goin' nowhere.

Jessie No school but. What ya gunna do Kyle?

Kyle Maybe burn somethin'.

Jessie Will not.

Kyle Steal somethin'.

Jessie Will not.

Kyle Kill somethin'.

Jessie Will not.

Kyle Get hit by a car.

Jessie You did that last year, Kyle.

Kyle Dunno yet. Dunno yet.

Jessie Gunna play with me Barbie I get for Christmas.

Kyle Will not.

> *Pause.*

Jessie 'Member that time we went on holidays to Nan's? 'Member that? We got the bus. 'Member that, Kyle? 'Member that baby possum Nan had? She found it in the roof 'n' she was takin' care of it 'cause it lost its mum? 'Member that?

Kyle Nuh.

Jessie Yeah ya do, Kyle, you was feedin' it. That was fun then. Nan said we was gunna live with her but then Dad come 'n' picked us up. 'Member that time, Kyle?

Kyle Nuh.

> *Pause.*

Jessie 'Member that time we went campin'?

Kyle Nuh.

Jessie Yeah, 'member Kyle?

Kyle Never went campin'.

Jessie Was like campin'. Mum 'n' me 'n' you 'n' Troy in your room. We all slept on the mattress 'n' we wouldn't let Dad in.

Kyle Wasn't campin'.

Jessie Mum said it was like campin'. Felt like campin'. I closed me eyes 'n' I thought I was campin'.

> *Pause.*

I got an idea, Kyle, I got an idea. Maybe we can go to Nan's. Kyle, maybe we can catch a bus to Nan's.

Kyle Too far. Cost too much.

Jessie Maybe we can.

Kyle We gotta wait in the car for Mum.

Pause.

Jessie Troy's sick, Kyle. He's all sleepy. Gotta find a phone, gotta try 'n' call home.

Kyle Got no money.

Jessie Saved me tuckshop.

Pause.

Kyle We gotta stay in the car, Jessie, Mum said.

Jessie Where is she, Kyle? Where's Mum? What if she's gone home? What if she forgot? Gotta find a phone.

Pause.

I'll go if you won't.

JESSIE packs up and gets out of the car.

She marches off into the dark.

Kyle Jessie, get back in the car

Jessie Gotta find a phone.

Kyle Get back in the car, Jessie.

Pause.

Jessie.

Pause.

I'll go.

JESSIE quickly turns around and comes back to the car.

Give us the five bucks. You wait in the car like Mum said.

Jessie Yes Kyle. I love you Kyle.

Kyle You get back in the car now, Jessie.

Jessie Yes Kyle.

KYLE waits for JESSIE to get back inside the car, then runs off into the dark.

Hoods He runs
   Dunlops flailing
   failing
   stripping him of speed
   imagining
   Nikes
   like winged heels on heroes
   flying free.

   Over the BP
   where inside the attendant
   distended with boredom
   endures his graveyard shift
   chugging down Pepsi slush
   by the bucket
   for sucrose kicks.

   Flying

   Over the old woman
   in her transparent nightdress
   in her brick veneer
   frail as fear
   peeking through louvres
   wrinkled hand poised
   on the telephone receiver.

   Flying

   Over the park
   where kids are spinning
   bingeing goon under a tree
   their fermented minds finding
   life's meaning
   in cask wine
   laughing when they see
   him passing in the sky.

   Flying

Over the underpass
where an old man sleeps
stinking of spirits
on a stained mattress
crawling with fleas
dreaming of a room
a bed
clean sheets.

Flying

Over the knitted pattern of
Christmas tree lights
woven like wool
into streets.
Then with his telescopic vision
he pins a yellow bird
shining bright.
A Nightowl
opened 24 hours every night.

'Flying...'

Earthbound

He switches off
his surround sound
aerial television
and descends.
Back on the suburban grid
of neon and bitumen
his Nikes
flight
ends.

> *The HOODS morph into KYLE and the NIGHTOWL MAN.*
>
> *KYLE walks across the entrance of the Nightowl store.*
>
> *He stands on the electronic buzzer alerting the NIGHTOWL MAN.*

Nightowl Man We got cameras in 'ere.
Kyle I need some change.
Nightowl Man Where's yer mum 'n' dad?

> *KYLE doesn't answer.*

On yer own are yer?

> *KYLE is silent.*

Cat got yer tongue?
Kyle I need some change.
Nightowl Man You gotta buy somethin' first. We got milk drinks,
packs of chips, sausage rolls, ice creams, Coca-Cola, pies, hotdogs,
donuts...

> *KYLE chooses a packet of chips.*
>
> *He places his five dollars on the counter.*
>
> *The NIGHTOWL MAN hands KYLE the change.*

Kyle Um, I need two twenties.
Nightowl Man Don't have any twenties left.
Kyle But that's what I need.
Nightowl Man You gotta make a phone call, do yer'? S'pose I might
have a twenty in my wallet. Yep, here's one, two. You want 'em?

Do yer'? Well come 'n' get 'em. Haven't got all night.

KYLE takes the money from the counter.

Hey, you wanna free Coke?

KYLE retreats.

That phone out front don't work, yer know. It's been broke for months. Tell yer what, you can use the one out back.

KYLE hesitates.

You need to use the phone or what?

KYLE moves forward to follow the NIGHTOWL MAN.

The NIGHTOWL MAN morphs into a HOOD.

Hoods   Pause.
It seems Jessie and Troy have flown too
with winged shoe
following their brother
traversing the star-studded skies
landing
here.

The HOOD morphs into JESSIE carrying baby Troy.

Jessie   Kyle.
Kyle   Told you to stay in the car, Jessie. Come on.

KYLE steals an armful of food from the shelves.

They run off.

Sound of a highway.

Give us yer hand.
Jessie   Wha'?
Kyle   Give us your hand, Jessie, we gotta cross the highway.

They hold hands and run.

They morph into the HOODS.

Hoods   Pause.
Headlights hunt them
pin them to bitumen.

Long-haul Mack truck blares its horn
screech of brakes
time stalls.
Pause.
Insert Special Feature.
Replay
seven a.m. yesterday.

Kids
munching cheese TV
recharging with sucrose fuel
cardboard cartoon cereal
sugared sweet.
Ten a.m. last day of school.
Mum still sleeps
sporting a mother bruise
on her left cheek.
She wakes up
in the ground-floor flat
splintered door
fist-punctured wall
recalls
this month's rent
due last week.
On the way to school
she finds a phone
and calls…

> *One of the HOODS morphs into MUM. She is in a public phonebox.*

Mum   Mum? Mum, it's me.

> *Silence.*

What else?

> *Silence.*

Mum, I spent the money you sent me.

> *Silence.*

No I didn't. I swear I didn't, Mum. They cut the phone off. In a phonebox. Kids are in the car. Can you give us some more? I'll pay yer back. Yeah, I'll come up. I will. I'll pack the car up now, pick the kids up after school. Yeah, I promise. I will.

Silence.

Will you stay up for us? 'Bye, Mum. See you soon.

Hoods She gets back
to the one-bedroom flat
packs.
Heaps her life into a Crazy Clark's bag
throws it in the car
slams the door.
In the blistering heat
falls asleep
and dreams of a life with more.
Three p.m.
she picks the kids up
drives to the supermarket
tells the kids
stay in the car.
Stop.
Enough of that day.
Fast-track it back
to the highway.

Long-haul Mack truck blares its horn.
Their fright
speeds their flight
turn left at the servo
car hoons past blaring stereo
through the dark
back to the carpark.

The HOODS become JESSIE and KYLE in the car.

KYLE and JESSIE stuff themselves with the food stolen from the Nightowl.

JESSIE spots a SECURITY GUARD patrolling the carpark.

Jessie   There's a security guard.

Kyle   Jessie, hide.

They duck and wait in silence until the SECURITY GUARD passes by.

Jessie   We should ask him for help.

Kyle   Won't help us.

Jessie   He'll help Troy.

Kyle   Don't need him.

Jessie   We should ask him.

JESSIE scrambles out of the car.

I'm gonna ask him.

Kyle   You leave, Jessie, I'll bash ya face in.

JESSIE stops still.

She turns and looks at KYLE.

Jessie   No ya won't.

Kyle   I will. I'll bash ya face in. Break ya arm off. Stab ya in the stomach.

Jessie   No ya won't.

Kyle   I will.

Jessie   Nuh, gunna ask him.

JESSIE walks away in the direction of the SECURITY GUARD.

Hoods   Pause.

Insert Special Feature.

Play.

Kyle   The title of me story is 'Me Frid'y'. I love Frid'ys. I love Frid'ys 'cause we get to have KFC. We always get a family pack which is for families. We eat our family pack in front of the tele, us four together. Sometimes Dad comes over 'n' eats some chips. Mum's go cold. 'Kids go to bed,' Dad says. But I don't wanna go to bed. I wanna stay in front of the tele all night. Don't want Fridy to end, don't want it to be tomorrow. He makes us go to bed. And then later, we come out, Mum's cryin' on the couch and our bags are packed and the car's runnin'.

Hoods Replay
every
other
Friday.

KYLE morphs into DAD and JESSIE morphs into MUM.

Dad It's all right, kids, I'm huggin' yer mum. See? Yer all right, aren't yer, Mum? Go on, tell 'em. Go on, tell 'em yer all right.

Mum Yeah, I'm all right, kids. I'm all right.

Dad Yer not goin' anywhere, Mum, are yer? Go on, tell 'em yer not goin' anywhere...

Mum I'm not goin' anywhere, kids. I'm not goin' anywhere.

MUM and DAD morph back into KYLE and JESSIE in the car.

Jessie We gotta find Nan's. We gotta find a bus.

Kyle Too far, Jessie, cost too much.

JESSIE pulls a crumpled, yellow envelope out of her pocket.

'It's all right, kids...'

36

She opens it and takes out a fifty-dollar note.

Where'd ya get that?

Jessie   Been savin' up.

Kyle   You stole it, didn't ya?

Jessie   No.

Kyle   You did. You stole it from Mum.

Jessie   Mr Mafeson gave it to me.

Kyle   Did not.

Jessie   Did too. He said I should save it for when I needed it. So I did, I kept it all year.

Jessie   Kyle, come on, we gotta go. The baby's cold.

Kyle   Can't leave Mum. What if she comes back?

Jessie   We'll leave a trail. She'll follow us to Nan's.

JESSIE opens up a chip packet and starts to make a trail of chips.

Come on, Kyle. Come on.

Kyle   Jessie, you get back in the car.

Jessie   I'm goin', Kyle. Come on.

Kyle   Jessie, you leave… Jessie, you leave…

KYLE takes the plastic bag out and threatens to pull it over his head.

Jessie   No, Kyle, gotta go. The baby's cold.

JESSIE is gone.

KYLE is alone in the carpark.

Kyle   Jessie. Jessie.

KYLE sits alone in the car.

Wish I was an Xbox, wish I was.

KYLE morphs into a HOOD.

Hoods   Stop.
Restart.

JESSIE appears in the carpark again.

Kyle   Can't leave Mum. What if she comes back?

JESSIE has an idea. She passes Troy to KYLE who holds him awkwardly.

Jessie We'll leave a trail. She'll follow us to Nan's.

JESSIE opens the packet of chips and starts to make a trail. She disappears into the darkness.

Kyle Where's Mum, Troy? Where's Mum?

Pause.

Mum's gone.

KYLE follows after JESSIE.

Jessie. Jessie, wait.

KYLE and JESSIE morph into the HOODS.

Hoods This is what happened.
Sun streaks
golden across the sky
folding up the dark
like last night's sheets
flinging out the stars.
Jessie lags
crumbling a salt and vinegar path
a connect-the-chips
edible zig-zag
but
a stray dog gobbles up the Samboy path
and
when Mum returns
finds
only the bag from Crazy Clark's
the car
empty
in the carpark.

Meanwhile

On a phone

outside a St Vinnie's depot
kids dial triple zero.
Waiting
near an overflowing green bin
dumped with unwanted things
broken couch
stuffing torn out
family of mice nesting in the springs.

Siren sings.
The baby
cold and heavy
breath rasping
survives
the long night's journey
changing everything.
And
in this ending
all three are free
flying
over the city
on a flight path to Nan's.

End game.

The HOODS carefully place the doll and other items back inside the Commodore.

They hear the pitbull's ferocious bark.

Chased by the dog, the HOODS run out of the wrecking yard, through the suburban streets and onto a train.

A suburban train station.

The HOODS board the train.

The sound of a train.

THE END

The Hoods ride the train.

REALtv is an artistic team that formed in late 2000. They have created new work for Queensland Theatre Company (*The Orphanage Project*, 2003), La Boite Theatre (*Kingswood Kids*, 2003), Queensland Arts Council (*Children of the Black Skirt*) and QPAT's Stage X Festival (*The Suitcase*, 2001). Real TV has received grants from Arts Queensland (2002 and 2001) and the Australia Council (2002). *Children of the Black Skirt*, Real TV's seminal work, has toured extensively with Queensland Arts Council to Queensland regional and metropolitan high schools. The popularity of *Children of the Black Skirt* resulted in a second regional tour of Queensland in 2004 and a subsequent tour throughout regional Victoria presented by Regional Arts Victoria. In 2005, the play toured South Australia as part of Adelaide's Come Out Festival for Young People, again to regional Victoria, and the work also enjoyed a season at the Sydney Opera House as part of the House:Ed program. The tour culminated in three performances in the Cape York Peninsula with Queensland Theatre Company. In 2005, *Children of the Black Skirt* was selected for the VCE Drama Studies Playlist and received a Drama Victoria Award for best production by a theatre company. The play has been published by Currency Press. *Hoods*, commissioned by Regional Arts Victoria and Sydney Opera House:Ed premiered in 2006 at the Sydney Opera House Studio. It subsequently toured metropolitan Queensland and regional Victoria. It was also presented at the Pacific Edge Conference in September and the Drama Vic Conference in November. In 2007, the production will tour Victoria, South Australia (Come Out Festival) and Queensland. The play has also been selected for the VCE Drama Studies Playlist for 2007. Real TV's mission is to produce outstanding political Australian stories for young audiences.

Angela Betzien
Playwright

Angela Betzien is an award-winning playwright. Her work, which has received several professional and independent productions, includes *Dog Wins Lotto* (Queensland Theatre Company, 1997), *Playboy of the Working Class* (Queensland Theatre Company, 2001), *The Suitcase* (Real TV/Stage X Festival, 2001), *Princess of Suburbia* (Real TV, 2001), *Kingswood Kids* (La Boite Theatre, 2002), *The Orphanage Project* (Queensland Theatre Company, 2003), *Children of the Black Skirt* (Queensland Arts Council and Real TV, 2003) and *Hoods* (commissioned by Sydney Opera House:Ed and Regional Arts Victoria, 2006). *Children of the Black Skirt* has been published by Currency Press. Angela was a member of the Queensland Theatre Company Board from 2003-06. She is also an experienced teacher of writing for theatre. She is currently working on a play about school as well as a new work for young audiences in collaboration with Arena Theatre and Sydney Opera House:Ed. She is also completing an MA (Playwriting) at Queensland University of Technology.

Leticia Cáceres
Director

Leticia Cáceres completed her tertiary education at QUT in 1999 where she received First Class Honours in Directing. In 2000, she was granted a mentorship with Queensland Theatre Company Artistic Director Michael Gow and co-founded Real TV. Her directing credits include *The Taming of the Shrew* (Shakespeare Festival, USQ, 2005), *Far Away* (QTC, 2004), *Something to Declare* (Actors for Refugees, 2004), *Children of the Black Skirt* (Real TV, 2003-05), *The Orphanage Project* (QTC, 2003), *Kingswood Kids* (La Boite, 2002) and *Princess of Suburbia* (Real TV, 2001). Leticia held the position of QTC Intern Director (2003) and QTC Associate Director in 2004. In 2005, she directed *The Memory of Water* for QTC, for which she received a Matilda Award nomination for Best Director. Also in 2005, she was awarded the BCC Lord Mayor's Fellowship, to study Direction in Argentina. She is currently the Artistic Director for Tantrum Theatre, Newcastle.

Pete Goodwin
Composer and Sound Designer

Pete Goodwin is a classically trained electronic composer, producer, performer, sound designer and DJ. His production outfit, Red light Disco (previously known as Smear), has been the forefront for his music since 1998, with several independent compact disc releases, as well as live multimedia performances both locally and nationally, including major Australian festivals. His theatre composition credits include seven productions for Queensland Theatre Company and all of Real TV's productions. Pete is currently working as a composer and sound designer on various independent film projects. Pete's website: www. redlightdisco.com

Jodie Le Vesconte
Performer

Jodie Le Vesconte has been a key artist with Real TV since its conception. She is a graduate of QUT (BA) Acting 1994, and received a performing arts scholarship to study at the Shakespeare & Company Summer Training Institute (Boston). She has appeared in numerous plays including *Constance Drinkwater and the Final Days of Somerset, The Memory of Water, The Orphanage Project, Phedra, The Threepenny Opera, Love Puke* (Queensland Theatre Company); *The Suitcase, Princess of Suburbia* and *Children of the Black Skirt* (Real TV); *The Man Who Sold the World, Macbeth, Unleashed* (Zen Zen Zo); *Wicked Bodies* and *Third World Blues* (La Boite Theatre); and *Dracula, Richard the Third* and *Scathac and Aoife* (Fractal Theatre). Jodie has received Light Globe and Del Arte Awards for her performances.

Christopher Sommers
Performer

Christopher is a graduate of QUT (BFA) Acting 2002. He has appeared most recently in the QTC Young Playwrights Awards, Restaged Histories' premiere of *Omon Ra* (Brisbane Powerhouse and Adelaide Fringe Festival), *Trivia* (Bunker Productions), La Boite Theatre's National Tour of *Zigzag Street* and *Sleeping Around* (Downstairs Belvoir), after making his professional debut in QTC'S award-winning *Proof*. Other credits include *The Oracle* (Brisbane Powerhouse) and *Stained* (Darlinghurst Theatre). Feature films include *Unfinished Sky* (New Holland Pictures), *All My Friends Are Leaving Brisbane* (Bunker Productions) and *The Horseman* (Kastle Films). Television credits include *Monarch Cove* (Grundy/Freemedia), *The Starter Wife* (NBC Universal) and *Love Bytes* (FOX 8). Short films include *Counter, Stray, This is Madonna* (Safezone Film Festival Finalist), *Doubt, Last Aussie Hero Trilogy, Crying Wolf* and the award-winning short *The Machine*.

Jonathon Oxlade
Designer

Jonathon Oxlade studied Illustration and Sculpture at the Queensland College of Art. Since leaving he has trained with Kid Praha in the Czech Republic focussing on puppet design and construction. He works as a freelance theatre designer, illustrator and puppeteer. He has designed set and costumes for *Live Acts on Stage* and *Baal* for Michael Gow and QUT; *Motor Mouth* for QPAC, QTC and Kite Theatre; *Where is Joy, Black Christmas* and *Brown* for independents; *Zoo-Illogical* for Kite Theatre; *Schnapper Head, Scribble for Brown Room* and *Bitin' Back* for Kooemba Jdarra and Wesley Enoch; *Sub-Con Warrior 1* for Zen Zen Zo; *Creche and Burn* and *The Dance of Jeremiah* for La Boite Theatre; *Show, Lily Can't Sleep, A Christmas Carol* and *Puss in Boots* for the Queensland Theatre Company; and *Lumina* for CIRCA. Jonathon has designed and made puppets for Queensland Theatre Company's *The Orphanage Project*; La Boite Theatre's *Half and Half* and *Ukulele Mekulele*; Divaldlo Continuo's *Kratochvilleni* (Prague); and for companies including Kite Theatre, Strut 'n' Fret, IZIT Entertainment and Theatre of Image.

Kylie Mitchell
Stage Manager / Production Manager

Kylie Mitchell is a graduate of the University of Southern Queensland. She has worked in various roles from stage, production and events management to lighting design. She has been involved with many of Queensland's performing arts companies including Queensland Theatre Company, La Boite, QPAC, Empire Theatre and the Powerhouse, as well as many up-and-coming independent theatre groups including Real TV and The Nest. Kylie undertook a residency as Stage Manager for JUTE in 2004 and is part of the events team at Southbank. In 2006, Kylie spent most of the year touring with Real TV on a successful season of *Hoods* as Stage and Tour Manager and has recently taken on the role of Production Manager for the company. Shows such as *The Knowing of Mary Poppins* and *Between Heaven and Earth* have seen Kylie cement her passion for production management.

♦ ♦ ♦ ♦ ♦

Also available from Currency Press:

Angela Betzien
CHILDREN OF THE BLACK SKIRT
Three lost children stumble across an abandoned orphanage in the bush. They become trapped in a timeless world, haunted by spirits from the past. They are tormented, too, by Black Skirt, a cruel governess who floats up and down the orphanage corridors wielding enormous scissors. But as the stories of these forgotten children are told—from pickpocketing incidents in the eighteenth century to the tragedies of the Stolen Generation in the twentieth—their spirits are released, one by one. *Children of the Black Skirt* is a gothic fairytale with bite. Roald Dahl meets Charles Dickens under the harsh Australian sun, as Angela Betzien explores Australia's history and the healing power of storytelling. Includes Teachers' Notes.
ISBN 978 0 86819 760 9

Philip Dean
AFTER JANUARY
Alex is marking time while awaiting his school results—body surfing, watching TV and playing pool are meanwhile his primary concerns. So he's not prepared for the girl with the nose-ring who cuts past him on a wave and draws him into a new way of looking at the world. Adapted from a novel by Nick Earls.
ISBN 978 0 86819 636 7

48 SHADES OF BROWN
In his final year at school, and with his parents overseas, Dan is forced to grow up fast when he moves in with his 22-year-old aunt Jacq and her eccentric friend Naomi. Light-hearted and funny, with a definite twist of insanity. Adapted from Nick Earls' novel.
ISBN 978 0 86819 652 7

Nick Enright

A PROPERTY OF THE CLAN

When a young girl is murdered at the hands of one of her male contemporaries, what is the aftermath? How will her friends cope? How can such violence be understood? Written for Freewheels TIE Theatre Co, *A Property of the Clan* deals with these issues with honesty, sensitivity and intelligence.
ISBN 978 0 86819 360 1

SPURBOARD

Greg spends his spare time gazing at the stars while his brother Mitchell prefers the mud of the rodeo arena. Karen and Amy are friends with wildly different ambitions. Juggling the demands of parents, friends and their own dreams, these four teenagers learn that adulthood begins with a voyage of self-discovery.
ISBN 978 0 86819 643 5

Margery Forde

X-STACY

Drawn by the power of the beat and the tribal escape of dance, Ben hangs out with Fergus, a choice rave DJ who is heading for the stars. For Zoe, an aspiring DJ, music is the drug and she's addicted. Ben's mother seeks rapture through the Church and the stories of the saints. When his younger sister, Stacy, wants to check out the rave scene, Ben knows he'll have to watch out for her. And tonight she's going to drop her first ecstasy pill. Later, Ben will struggle to forgive himself and his mother retreats into the Church. But the time will come to face the truth about what really happened that night.
ISBN 978 0 86819 602 2

Ross Mueller

COLOSSEUM

A multi-plotted play written for an ensemble cast of at least fifteen actors, for characters aged between thirteen and twenty-five. Ben and Liam are importers who accidentally receive a shipment of religious statues, unaware of what is hidden inside. Rich works at the docks and is tied up in too many deals. Sonia is an usher at the cinema, cleaning up after people like Samantha, a

final year med student who spends too much time at the movies and who studies mechanics with Belinda, a cleaner who believes in self-improvement and dreams of becoming a pop star. Belinda cleans houses with Peta, who yearns for the revolution. Fifteen lives intersect as this multi-layered story explores life's infinite possibilities.
ISBN 978 0 86819 693 0

Richard Oxenburgh and Andrew Ross
THE MERRY-GO-ROUND IN THE SEA
'His life had no progression back in town, the days led nowhere. He woke in the morning in his room, and at night he slept; the wheel turning full circle, the merry-go-round of his life revolving.'

The year is 1941, Australian soldiers are fighting overseas and in Geraldton locals dig air raid trenches in their backyards, just in case. Six-year-old Rob Coram idolises his enigmatic older cousin Rick, but his idyllic existence on the west coast of Australia is disrupted when Rick volunteers for active service. Interned by the Japanese, Rick struggles to survive, just as Rob will struggle to overcome the void created by Rick's absence and to understand the disillusioned man who returns. Adapted by Dickon Oxenburgh and Andrew Ross from Randolph Stow's classic novel, *The Merry-Go-Round in the Sea* captures the restless spirit of post-war Australia.
ISBN 978 0 86819 788 3

Visit the new Currency Press website for
extensive Teachers' Notes on
Hoods

www.currency.com.au

CURRENCY PRESS
The performing arts publisher

PO Box 2287, Strawberry Hills, NSW 2012, Australia
Tel: (02) 9319 5877   Fax: (02) 9319 3649
E-mail: enquiries@currency.com.au